Katy's Gift

Katy's Gift

By Keith Bowen

With Dan Gutman

AN IMPRINT OF RUNNING PRESS
PHILADELPHIA • LONDON

9   8   7   6   5   4   3   2   1
Digit on the right indicates the number of this printing

71603
Library of Congress Cataloging-in-Publication Number 96-~~72568~~

ISBN 0-7624-0169-9

Edited by Tara Ann McFadden

This book may be ordered by mail from the publisher. Please include $2.50
for postage and handling. ***But try your bookstore first!***

Published by Courage Books, an imprint of
Running Press Book Publishers
125 South Twenty-second Street
Philadelphia, Pennsylvania 19103-4399

To my mother
—K. B.

Katy and Amos Stoltzfus wake up before the Pennsylvania sun. Today is market day, and the family must buy hay for their horse, Jed. The Stoltzfus family is Amish. They don't drive cars, watch television, or have telephones in their homes. They prefer to live simply. But sometimes, even for Amish children, life is not so simple.

Father goes off to the hay auction, while Mother takes Katy and Amos to buy supplies. Suddenly, Katy spies a toy wooden rocking horse, brightly painted and shiny. She can't take her eyes off it. It is the most beautiful thing she has ever seen.

"I would love to have a little rocking horse like that," Katy whispers to Amos.

"Five dollars," says the woodcarver.

"Five dollars is a lot of money," says Amos, as he and Katy have a snack.

"Maybe I can make a quilt and sell it," Katy says.

"That would take months, or even years," Amos says.

"Maybe I can enter Jed in a race and win the money."

"Jed is old and slow," Amos laughs.

Father comes back with a load of hay. "It is time to get back to the farm and do chores," he tells the children.

The children work hard at their
chores, but Katy is still thinking about
how she might earn enough money
to buy the little wooden horse.

"Maybe I could sell a few of the
chicken's eggs," she suggests.

"Mam would be upset,"
Amos warns.

"Is it wrong, Mam, to want something so badly that you can't think of anything else?"

"No," Mother replies as she and Katy clean the house. "But sometimes you can't have everything your heart desires."

"Dat," Amos asks his Father as
they feed and milk the cows,
"may I have five dollars so that I
can buy my sister something she
really wants?"

"No," Father replied. "I am pleased
that you care about your sister, but
money is something we must earn."

Some people think the Amish
don't do anything but work all day.
Actually, Amish children love to
play games, too. After lunch, Katy
and Amos ride the swing that hangs
from the tree in their backyard.
They also like to play baseball, cuddle
their kittens, and even rollerblade!

Amos loves to ride his scooter. Near the covered bridge, the scooter's wheel suddenly hits a rock, and Amos tumbles to the ground. The wheel is shattered.

Katy invites Amos to take a ride on her tricycle. They have fun together, but Katy knows Amos feels sad about his scooter.

Pumpkins and gourds are grown on the farm, and now it's harvest time. Katy's afternoon chore is to arrange them neatly at the end of the drive. People passing by take the ones they want and leave money in a tin cup.

Katy sees there are still some small gourds scattered in the field.

"What about these gourds, Mam?" she asks.

"They are too tiny," Mother says. "People won't want them."

"May I try to sell them, please?"

"If you wish."

Katy collects the unwanted gourds in a basket and
carefully makes a sign: Baby gourds, ten cents each.

The next morning, Katy rushes
outside to see if anyone bought her
little gourds. She looks in the
basket, and it is empty.

The tin cup she left next to the basket is filled almost to the brim with coins. Carefully, Katy counts them. The total is five dollars and fifty cents.

Katy just about shouts with joy. "Now I have enough money to buy the wooden horse!" She has never been so happy in her life.

"Dat, can we go to the woodcarver's shop?" Katy pleads. "I want to buy something with the money I earned."

"First we must get a new horseshoe for Jed. Some things are more important than others," Dat likes to say.

In the blacksmith's shop, Katy spots a wheel exactly like the one on Amos's scooter.

"Five dollars," says the blacksmith.

Katy thinks it over for a long time. Finally she decides that her father is right—some things are more important than others. The wooden horse would be nice to play with, but Amos needs his scooter more.

"I'd like to buy that wheel, please," she tells the blacksmith.

Father puts the new wheel on the scooter and Amos races up and down the yard, kicking up clouds of dust. He is so thankful, he wants Katy to take a ride.

It makes Katy feel good to know that she made Amos happy. At the same time, she thinks about the wooden horse, and that makes her feel a little sad.

Soon it will be suppertime. Katy helps her mother prepare chicken, potatoes, and vegetables. All of which were grown right on the farm.

Amos rushes to give the mules and horses enough hay and water for the night. He is especially fast tonight because he wants to meet a friend before supper.

The Stoltzfus family gathers in the kitchen and sits at the table. They all bow their heads and say a silent prayer. The sweet smell of mashed potatoes makes everyone hungry.

"Katy," says Mother, as she slaps a heaping spoonful of steaming potatoes on a plate, "that was so kind of you to use your money to give a gift to Amos."

"I have a gift for you too, Katy," Amos says as he gets up from the table.

Amos returns carrying the wooden horse that Katy wanted so badly.

"This is the nicest present I have ever received!" Katy says gleefully. "Where did you get five dollars, Amos?"

"I sold my scooter," Amos says.

"What?" protests Katy.

"Some things are more important than others."

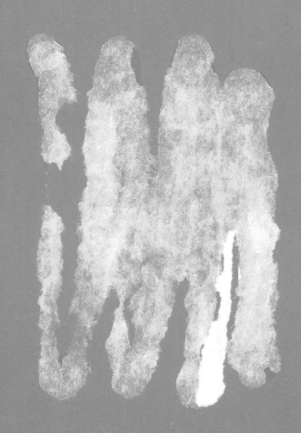